Olive

Original Poems

Olive

Original Poems

ISBN/EAN: 9783337398187

Printed in Europe, USA, Canada, Australia, Japan

Cover: Foto ©Andreas Hilbeck / pixelio.de

More available books at **www.hansebooks.com**

ORIGINAL POEMS.

Preface.

HESE poems were printed two years ago for sale for a local charitable purpose, but the book could not be got ready in time for a particular Bazaar. Many friends of the authoress have expressed their disappointment at the non-production of the poems they knew I had proposed publishing. I have, therefore, acceded to their wishes by ordering this little book to be brought out now in the state in which I left it. It may possess interest, beyond the circle of the acquaintance of the authoress, as shewing a result of education in a village school before the passing of the Elementary Education Act. My attention was first called to "Olive's" poems by verses I had seen written in newspapers containing local allusions to my own neighbourhood. I found, on inquiry, that they were written by the youngest daughter of one of my father's tenants, who had been educated at Linley School, and that she had become a regular contributor to a London as well as to provincial publications. With respect to the poems, they are not revised by any other hand than her own, beyond my marking a few lines in which the metre required improvement, but the lines, thus altered, are "Olive's" own. There is a poem in the middle of the book which I wished to be exchanged for some other, but no new poem was received before the whole was printed.

Two poems at the end of the book, describe traditions well known on the Montgomeryshire Border of Shropshire. The first, on the "Robber's Grave," tells the story written in prose by the Rev. Mostyn Pryce. It was the fact that for many years after the alleged sheep-stealer's execution, grass did not grow on his grave, as he prayed it might not, in proof of his innocence. It might of course be suggested that the inhabitants or friends of the man were interested in preventing the growth of grass on the grave. The grave, however, may be seen in Montgomery Churchyard, and I have not found any local testimony favour the suggestion that artificial means were used to establish the man's innocence in accordance with his dying prayer.

The poem of "Maggie's Pinfold," describes a well-known tradition connected with a circle of stones near Corndon, which may also be seen by any one who has the curiosity to visit a spot well worthy of a visit. The story of the Lake, which appears in another poem, is, of course, a tale of the North, and not connected with Shropshire.

R. JASPER MORE.

June, 1874.

Original Poems.

PART I.

The Poet.

WHAT is a poet? not some wondrous thing,
   But just a person you may meet with often
In daily life; who does his best to sing,
   The ruggedness of his own lot to soften.

Who goes his way and does his work as well,
   As if he heard no pleasant echoes ringing,
From that far land where none but poets dwell,
   With nought to mar the sweetness of their singing.

Who, though he loves to notice birds and flowers,
   Can yet plan out and do a good day's labour,
Who thinks it not beneath his mental powers,
   To do his duty and respect his neighbour.

This is a poet; and 't is such as he,
   Who, though the great ones pass them all unheeding,
Though hard their hands and small their learning be,
   Make their whole lives a poem worth GOD's reading!

An Invocation.

Shine, crystal moon, where the river's sweet flow
   Creeps through the alders that grow by my home;
Beam, golden stars, as in years long ago,
   Forth from your watch-towers in Heaven's high dome.

Blow, western wind, o'er the green clover lea,
   Sigh through the aspens your old summer chime,
Weave the same chants that were music to me
   When my heart was so light in that mystic spring-time.

Sing, happy bird, in the white cherry bloom,
   Float through the rosy-tipped orchards away,
Till your carol is lost in the wood's leafy gloom,
   And its echo dies out with the vanishing day.

Come, joyous Spring, with your old sunny glow,
   Gladden the earth with your sunshine and rain,
But can ye restore me the lost "long ago?"
   Can ye bring, can ye bring me my childhood again?

In Memory of Reb. T. F. M.

Once more we gather round the blazing hearth —
   Not with the careless glee of other years —
A gloom has fallen on our Christmas mirth,
   And dimmed our glowing holly-wreath with tears.

For one has passed from out this troublous scene,
   A noble heart whom we would fain have kept;
Old men have mourned his death, and tears have been
   In eyes that have not since their childhood wept.

For he was one who knew the varied strings
   Of life's great harp; to wake its lowest tone
Into sweet music, and to common things
   To give a grace and sweetness of his own.

When death or sickness visited a home,
   His was the hand that pointed us above,
That led us weeping from the grave's dark gloom,
   And pierced the clouds that veiled a Father's love.

To those who stumbled in rough duty's path,
 IIis loving heart with warm compassion stirred ;
From him they had no threats of coming wrath,
 But prayers, and many a kind consoling word.

The laugh of little children was to him
 Sweeter than that applause which courts the great,
Like echoes from the songs of seraphim,
 Floating at eve through heaven's half-open gate !

In him the widow and the fatherless
 Have lost a brother and a faithful friend,
Whose bounty, like his love, was fathomless,
 Whose sympathising kindness knew no end.

And now we lay him sadly in the ground,
 Having no words our sorrow to reveal,
Knowing how far above all voice or sound
 Is that deep grief which all around us feel.

O, Thou ! to whom this feeble prayer shall come,
 Through shining angel-ranks and starry spheres,
Grant that we, too, may reach that far-off home,
 And spend with him heaven's long, eternal years !

Finley Wood.

The breeze sighs through the leafy wood;
   I love to turn away,
And lose in this green solitude
   The cares of every day:

For other feelings may grow cold,
   And other fancies range,
But Nature greets us as of old—
   Her love will never change.

Such dreams as happy childhood weaves
   Come back to cheer me now;
As then, the shining beech-tree leaves
   Bend down to touch my brow.

Around me grows the drooping birch,
   The fir-tree's graceful pride;
The sombre pine and graceful larch
   Rise stately, side by side.

And sweetly glancing through their gloom,
By contrast yet more fair,
The mountain ash, whose snowy bloom
Has sweetened all the air.

Beneath the fern the rabbit flits,
A happy life has he;
Amongst the boughs the squirrel sits,
And chatters forth his glee.

And green the honeysuckle wreaths
Around the branches twine;
The pale wild rose its perfume breathes
O'er clustering tufts of thyme.

The oak-trees' mighty arms outspread,
The sunlight glints between,
The woodlark singeth over head
In his sweet world of green.

Instead of restless, hurrying feet,
The soft wind wanders by;
And through the boughs I watch a fleet
Of cloud-ships in the sky.

And these are with me all day long,
To light my working hours:
The winds' low sigh, the wild birds' song,
The greenwood's leaves and flowers.

SECOND PART.

Linley Wood 's in all its glory,
When old autumn passes through—
Golden, crimson, brown, and hoary,
Every tree a different hue.

Some their pleasant green remaining,
Some grown sere with early frost,
Some whose wondrous tinted veining
Make all artist-labour lost.

Sloping down the "coppice dingle,"
Trees of all the forest grow:
There the colours meet, and mingle
In a ripe, delicious glow.

Slender birch and silvery willow,
Maple saplings straight and tall,
Oaks and larches, elms and beeches,
Solemn firs amongst them all.

Like a flame the red is stealing
  Down the avenue of beech,
Whose gray trunks are carved and tattered,
  High as boyish hands can reach.

Further, where the great, dark pine trees
  Hold dominion of their own,
The sad Spirit of the Forest
  Sighs and whispers all alone.

And, like music heard in dreaming,
  Floating forth in echoes low,
Comes an answer through the gloaming,
  From the brook's harmonious flow;

Sweet and mystic are its numbers,
  Yet by poets understood,
Winding 'neath the round-leaved alders,
  By the shades of Linley Wood.

O the glory of the woodlands!
  O the beauty of the skies!
O the grandeur of the mountains,
  As the summer faints and dies!

Nature's best and choicest beauties,
Forest, hills, and waters meet,
Where old Rhadley smiles so proudly
On the meadows at his feet.

Many a cottage, neat and nest-like,
Many an open, pleasant farm,
Leads to where the white church-steeple
Gives to all a sacred charm.

In the Woods.

"Peace! peace!" the waving trees do say—
"Peace! peace!" my heart replies.—*Anon.*

Green waving trees! ye are so dear to me,
Your quiet presence hath so strange a charm,
That I have even prayed
Beneath your solemn shade
That I might lay my head upon my arm,
And die, forgetting all the cares that be.

Then many a tinted leaf and fragrant bell
Should drop its tears upon the passing breeze;
The ringdove's plaintive note
Should through the stillness float,
And, more than all, the green, majestic trees
Should mourn for one who loved them dearly well.

The light and shade would play upon my face,
As now they dance about the ground I tread;
Green tufted fern-leaves there
Should wave in scented air;
The wild rose and the hawthorn bough should shed
Their blossomed sweetness o'er my resting-place.

To no more tears my wearied eyes should wake,
But in the stillness of the summer eves
The soft stars looking through
From their great arch of blue,
Should find me lying 'neath a roof of leaves,
In such a calm as sorrow could not break.

Oh! Death! that gatherest the fair young flowers,
But heedest not the prayers of weary men,
I pray thee that if thou
Coldly pass by me now,
Yet hear my prayer, and kindly take me when
My soul is purified by those calm hours!

PART II.

Where art Thou?

Thinking of thee when at twilight I stray,
  Where the night breezes come cool to my brow;
Thinking of thee through the long busy day,
  Silently wondering "Where art thou now?"
It may be thy soul is in sadness and woe;
  Wearied with sorrow thy spirit may bow:
Would I might comfort thee—would I might know,
  E'en as the angels do, where thou art now.
Far from thee earthward, my pathway must tend,
  Yet, when the seal of death rests on this brow,
Then shall I meet thee, and love thee, my friend;
  Then shall I never sigh "Where art thou now?"

On reading the Life of Keats.

 heart that nothing false comes nigh,
  A love for all things pure and sweet,
A poet's soul, an artist's eye—
  Alas for him in whom they meet!
For busy men will never own
  A fellowship with things so high ;
Great souls most often live alone,
  We only love them when they die.

Such was his fate who now is gone :
  He worked with faith from day to day,
And hoped and waited for the dawn,
  When purer creeds shall have their sway.
But hard it was for him to learn,
  From careless look or taunting speech,
How deaf an ear the world will turn
  To thoughts whose source it cannot reach.

Till wounded by the scorn he met,
  And failing in the work he tried,
Himself against the world he set,
  And threw his half-done tasks aside.
Awhile he lived a loveless life ;
  Then as a wearied child lies down,
So did he pass from out the strife,
  And so resigned his earthly crown.

Of him, now he is with the dead,
  Men speak thus kindly : " Had we known
How pure a light his spirit shed,
  How much more love we might have shown."
Of him the angels in their bliss
  Say sadly, " 'T is in vain we lend
To earth a soul so high as this,
  Whose worth they could not comprehend."

In the Valley of the Shadow of Death.

To die: to be forgotten, and to lie
In the lone grave, where all will pass me by,
Careless and heedless of who lies below,
Oh, it is hard! I do not wish to go,
To leave the busy world—the anxious race
In which I hoped so soon to take my place.
Yet I have never tried to write my name
With iron pen upon the scroll of fame.
But I have longed, with earnest longings, too,
The painful path of duty to pursue;
To do some good, some lonely ones to cheer,
To leave some record of my being here,
In kindly deeds and acts of mercy shown
To those whose paths were rougher than my own.
And now to die. My resting-place will be
Under the shadowy arms of some old tree.
The autumn's golden leaves, the winter snows
Will fall unheeded, and the step of those

Whom I have loved will pass unnoticed by;
And when they come to gaze on where I lie,
I shall not know it. Oh, how hard it seems
To realise the vague, uncertain dreams
We have of the hereafter. I alone
Must venture forth to meet the dread unknown,
And no loved voice—no kindly clasping hand—
Will come to reassure me when I stand
Trembling upon the brink of that cold sea
That flows between Eternity and me.
Now I look back on moments that have flown—
Charmed hours, in which my happy soul hath known
A joy as exquisite—a bliss as sweet
As throbs the hearts of angels when they meet
In distant bowers of Paradise. I know
That I have set my love too much below;
That I have loved the beautiful and grand
Of earth and sky, unmindful of the Hand
That made them so; my highest thoughts were given
Too much to earth and not enough to heaven;
Seeking on earth rewards which are above,
I acted uprightly to win men's love.
O but to live those wasted years again,
To undo that which I have done in vain!

At Rest.

So full of light and life she seemed,
　So blithe and glad from day to day,
No wonder those about her deemed
　That heart and brow alike were gay.
For she was one who could not bear
　That careless eyes should read her heart,
To smile at fears they could not share,
　And hopes in which they had no part.

And while she smiled they did not know
　She hid her hope's fresh-covered grave,
Far, far beneath that transient glow,
　As rocks are hidden 'neath the wave:
And even as those rocks are worn
　And broken by the waves' light play,
So 'neath her brightness did she mourn
　Till her young life ebbed all away.

And then, with kind and tender hand,
    Death claimed what long had been his own,
And took her to the "Silent Land,"
    Where she no more should feel alone.
The elms their ghostly branches wave
    Above the spot where now she sleeps;
And thickly strewed above her grave
    The yellow leaves lie dead in heaps.

A Prayer.

Lead me to Thee, O Father! for my feet
Are sorely wearied in the noon-day heat;
Fain would I rest beneath Thy mercy seat.
Lead me to Thee!

Only by GOD the chains can be unwound,
By which this struggling soul to earth is bound;
O seek me, Father, while I may be found.
Lead me to Thee!

Wide is the wilderness wherein I stray,
Sin holds and leads me further every day,
In mercy hear me, Father, when I pray.
Lead me to Thee!

My darkened soul is only half awake,
Let Thy great love, like morning, o'er it break,
And chase these shadows. O, for Jesu's sake,
Lead me to Thee!

Thou knowest, Lord, I have not glorified
Thee with my youth; but rather sought and tried
All things and thoughts that could yield joy beside.
All my first love to one of earth was given—
If that had stood, I had not thought of heaven:
It failed; and now, all desolate and riven,
My spirit turns and cries to be forgiven.
Falling and fainting on the world's highway,
The broken reeds which once I made my stay,
Pierce through my soul: O hear me while I pray,
Lead me to Thee!

Thou saidst of old, "I am a jealous GOD:"
Not so, my Father, for these feet have trod
In paths that led the furthest from Thy shrine;
This heart has owned all other love than Thine;
These hopes have been, not for Thy peace, O Lord,
But the good will of man, the scant award
Of praise that human justice could afford.
And now, bereft of that I prized so much,
Bent down with sin, whose bitterness is such
Those dream not of who meet me every day,
I come to Thee in solitude to pray,
Give me Thy lighter yoke, Thine easier way,
Lead me to Thee!

The End we hope for.

Have ye not heard that in that far bright home,
  Where Life's pure river glides,
Where never shade of human grief can come,
  Where lasting joy abides,

That those shall meet, a re-united band,
  Whom earth had parted far,
Heart reading heart, and hand close-clasping hand,
  Where none but pure things are?

That never any cloud of fear or doubt
  Shall come to grieve them there,
But CHRIST's pure love shall gird them all about,
  And GOD's protecting care.

That never any memory of the tears
  And griefs they have passed through
Shall come to them through those eternal years
  To vex their souls anew.

And then their eyes, unclouded by life's cares,
  Shall learn all mysteries—
Why were unheeded those impatient prayers,
  Those passionate outcries,

Which they have made, scarce knowing what they asked;
  And CHRIST shall pour sweet balm
On troubled souls, and weary hearts o'ertasked
  Shall find perpetual calm.

PART III.

The Deserted House.

A SILENCE still and deep, as if the wings
Of solitude drooped o'er the lonely spot;
On rusted hinge the broken wicket swings;
Fearless, beside the door, the wild bird sings,
And rabbits scamper through the garden plot.

In the green fields that lie beneath the hill,
The pheasant trails his brown and golden plume,
The grass grows long and rank beside the sill,
The house is left, deserted, lone, and still,
Surrounded by a silence and a gloom.

The chestnut tree that grows beside the door,
　　Holds forth its blossoms in their white array;
The green leaves seem to droop in sadness o'er,
Because the hands of children nevermore
　　Shall pluck those flowers to make the window gay!

The house is left; no more at break of day
　　Shall wreaths of smoke curl through the branches green;
The household gods and fairies, which, men say,
Dwell by each fireside, sadly turn away,
　　Sighing to think what comfort they have seen.

And nevermore the pleasant wood shall ring
　　With laughter clear, and merry, childish calls;
Henceforth the house will be a lonely thing,
Although, like ivy, tender memories cling
　　To these waste floors, and dead, deserted walls.

Summer.

When summer brings the roses,
    At first her steps are slow;
Her beauty she discloses
    In glades and valleys low.

In leafy nooks bestowing
    Her presence, half concealed,
As though afraid of showing
    Her charms at once revealed.

Low down in mossy dingles,
    Where blackbirds build and sing,
She dawneth first, and mingles
    Her flowers with those of Spring.

But ere we miss the sweetness
    That haunts the steps of May,
She comes in full completeness,
    In all her fair array.

No longer half beholden,
But gaily shining forth;
In emerald robes and golden
She decks the joyful earth.

A bounteous hand she reaches
Across the grassy plain;
The soaring lark she teaches
A new and sweeter strain.

She lingers where the streamlet,
Its daisied brinks between
Trickles, or down the hillsides
Where ferns are waving green.

Amongst the grey rock ledges
A fresh perfume she breathes;
She veils the thorny hedges
With hop and bindweed wreaths.

With no bare spot neglected,
She works with silent speed,
Till beauty is perfected,
And Summer reigns indeed.

The Chesnut Tree.

Before my window grows a tree,
　　In which all day the wild bees hum,
And music and perfume to me
　　It beareth when the blossoms come.
And every year its flowers of white
　　Like silver candelabra grow ;
Deep in their hearts one spot of light
　　Gleams like a rose leaf dropped on snow.

Amongst its boughs the blackbird's song
　　First echoes on the soft spring air ;
And when the summer days are long,
　　The starlings come to whistle there.
The linnet sits and warbles late,
　　Till sunset clouds have left the sky,
And there the swallows congregate
　　To chirp " farewell " before they fly.

And when the birds and flowers are gone,
    I think I love it more the while
The tender moonlight lingers on
    Its branches, like an angel's smile.
Thus autumn sere or leafy spring
    Are each in turn most dear to me,
For all the changing seasons bring
    Fresh beauty to my chesnut tree.

Mary and I.

The moon's shining bright o'er the hill's rugged steep,
The world looks as though it were lying asleep;
I am sitting alone with a pen in my hand,
And a book on my desk that I can't understand;
So my much-troubled thoughts have flown back with a sigh
To the long-vanished childhood of Mary and I.

I smile to remember the frolicsome times,
Ere she wore long dresses, or I tried at rhymes—
Ere the "black ox" of trouble had set his great feet
On the blossoms that grew in our life-garden sweet;
And we longed for the time that should crown our full cup
With the dignified title of being "grown up."

What rambles as blackberry-hunters we took,
What excursions we made with our long nutting-hook,
What tumbles we had in the sweet-scented hay,
Oh, our lives were as bright as the long summer day!
You are proud, Mary dear, but I think you would fain
Yield it all to be called "little Polly" again.

How we used to look forward, as only girls can,
With our three chosen friends, Patty, Bessie, and Anne,
To the time when the shackles of childhood should fall,
And we should be women, "nice-looking and tall,"
And the world should be bright as a fairy-land round—
But a sterner reality each of us found.

For Annie lies low in a far foreign grave,
Where the woods of New Zealand all distantly wave,
Where the low utter'd growl of the tiger's red throat
Replies to the boom of the bittern's harsh note ;
And the foot of the Indian stealthily creeps
O'er the grave where the dust of our dear playmate sleeps.

And Patty, the joyous and gay little thing,
Who joined our game "touch-wood," or "kiss-in-the-ring,"
Has been married this three years, quite matronly grown,
And important, with children and cares of her own.
Even Bessie is graver than in days gone by,
And all are more altered than Mary and I.

PART IV.

The Robber's Grave.

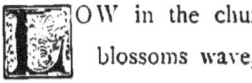OW in the churchyard, green and fair, where leaves and
blossoms wave,
Is shown a strip of barren earth, 't is called the "Robber's Grave."
From other graves it lies remote, no turfy mound is near;
No letter'd stone is there to tell the sadly-closed career,
Yet oft the traveller's footsteps pause, and children linger there
With simple awe to hear the tale of why the grave is bare.
Tradition says that eighty years their chequered course have run
Since near Montgomery's ancient town a reckless crime was done;

The robbers laid their plot so well, that while unharmed they fled,
The burden of their wicked act fell on a guiltless head.
A deftly-woven tale of guilt but all too smoothly ran,
And soon the law's most harsh decree condemned the friendless
man.

And he, as one tired out with life, in meekness bowed his head,
But ere he met his awful doom these words prophetic said :
"Confession of my sins I make to God, and Him alone ;
My perfect innocence of this hereafter shall be known.
Life hath but little charm for me ; there is but one I leave
Who loves me, branded as I am, for her dear sake I grieve;
And for the sake of her alone I wish to clear my name,
That she may know the heart she prized was free, at least, from
shame.
And God will grant this prayer, that all my innocence may see,
My grave, for more than forty years, a barren spot shall be,
And not a blade of grass thereon its dewy head shall bow,
Unless ye find the man for whose dark crime I suffer now."

Twice forty years have passed since then, the grave may yet be
seen,
All sterile, bare, and desolate, amid surrounding green ;

Though she of whom he spoke had brought full many a root
and stem —
In vain! the earth which covered him refused to succour them;
And though she watched them morn and eve, they withered every
one,
And ne'er a flower expanded there its beauties to the sun.
She knew that he was innocent, whate'er the world might say,
And for his sake alone she trod life's dull, unequal way.
And men with saddened eyes pass by that barren spot of ground;
Still stands the gray old church, and still on all the graves around
The roses blush and fuchias trail, and grasses richly wave,
But never leaf or blade has grown above the Robber's Grave!

Mitchell's Fold, near Corndon.

Once through the land, the old folks say, a mighty famine spread,
Old age and tender infancy died out for lack of bread,
And brave, strong men grew pale with want and hollow-eyed
 with grief,
To see their dear ones suffering when there was no relief.
No more the labourer's happy song woke with the summer's morn,
No more the farmer's wide-stretched fields stood thick with full-
 eared corn ;
For cruel famine ruled the land, and want's relentless ire
Had long since hushed the children's laugh and damped the
 cottage fire.
But there were fairies in those days (I wish there were some now),
And one came through the country then, and brought with her
 a cow —

A snow-white cow, whose shape and size old people speak of
still,
And closed her in the circle of grey stones on Stapeley Hill,
And bade the starving peasant wives each night and morning go
With one pail each, and milk, she said, should never cease to
flow.
What words can tell the joy with which this bounty was received!
What weakly lives grew strong again! what misery was relieved!
And how they bless'd the fairy cow, who had such ample store,
That e'en where crowds were satisfied would yield one pailful
more.
Now, in the country dwelt a witch, an ill-disposed old crone,
Who practised not the good advice of "letting well alone;"
Besides, it grieved her that, although she had in sorcery dealt,
The people had not sought her aid when this distress was felt.
So for their harm she wrought her spells, but vainly tried them
o'er,
Till she recalled the fairy's words, "One pailful each, no more."
Then with fell glee she took her pail, the bottom broke away,
And placed a sieve where it had been, and started off, they say,
Before the sunrise lit the earth, or any one was near,
To see that she so drew the milk that it might disappear.
And by this means the spell was loosed, the white cow sank
away

Down through the ground, but in the stones the witch was
    forced to stay;
And when the thronging people came they found the woman
    there
With her false pail—the much-loved cow they saw not anywhere.
They saw the wasted milk, and then knew what the witch had
    done,
So walled her up and left her in that living tomb of stone.
The famine passed: but still this tale is in the country told,
Of how the witch was starved to death, walled up in Mitchell's
    Fold.

Lake Semerwater.

(A LEGEND OF WENSLEYDALE, YORKSHIRE.)

Green grows the fern on Fleet-moss Wold,
    And brown the mantling heather ;
The harebells blue and furze-bloom gold
    Blend sweetly there together.
And nature spreads in flowery pride
    The robes which June has brought her ;
Where Bain's untroubled wavelets glide
    Into Lake Semerwater.

The breeze through ash and beechen bowers
    Blows soft when eve is closing,
And rocks the lily's waxen flowers,
    Upon the tide reposing.
Gay with the blackbird's echoing tones,
    And calmed by dusk of even,
The twilight star looks down and owns
    'T is almost fair as heaven.

Yet legends say this peaceful scene
    Is but of late creation ;
That once these grassy glades have been
    A waste and desolation.
Of old, they say, a thriving town
    Stood where these waves are flowing,
And streets are hidden where, far down,
    The lily roots are growing.

And once a weary, aged man
    Came through that olden city,
And vainly asked of those he saw
    For food and rest, in pity.
But all so cold their hearts had grown
    With cares and fashions splendid.
The houseless man passed on alone,
    Faint, worn, and unbefriended.

Outside the town a cottage stood.
    The home of shepherd Malcolm.
Who took him in and gave him food.
    And rest, and warmth, and welcome.
Next morning, standing at the door,
    He looked toward the city,

And raised his hand, and murmured o'er
    The words of this strange ditty :

" Semerwater rise, Semerwater sink,
    And bury the town, all save the house
Where they gave me meat and drink."

And straightway then the waters rose
    From out the brown earth gushing ;
From where the river Bain now flows
    Came heavy torrents rushing,
And buried all the busy town,
    And drowned the helpless people ;
" Full fathoms five" the billows flowed
    Above the great church steeple.

And still when boating on the lake
    When sunset clouds are glowing,
The roofs and spires may yet be seen
    Beneath the waters showing.
But on the shepherd's house, they say,
    The old man left his blessing ;
And so they prospered every day,
    With flocks and herds increasing.

Nor did it rest with them alone,
　But reached to son and daughter,
Until the land was all their own
　About Lake Semerwater.

Little Lizzie.

When the day is softly closing,
   And the sun is in the west;
When, as if with brightness wearied,
   Birds and blossoms sink to rest;
Then I have the sweetest pleasure
   That can crown a day of care,
When, with folded hands, my darling
   Kneels to say her evening prayer.

Ah! it is so sweet to see her,
   With her little serious face,
And her earnest eyes uplifted
   With such reverential grace.
Like a crown of light celestial
   Shines her falling golden hair —
Surely angels bend to listen
   To my darling's evening prayer.

"Our Father!" so she murmurs;
    And the thought is so divine
That it calms a troubled spirit —
    "*Our* Father!"—hers and mine.
She, so young, so fair, and spotless—
    Human, yet so free from sin;
I, so far away from heaven—
    She, so fit to enter in.

Little Lizzie, pure and gentle,
    Keep thy "hallowed evening prayers;"
Life may some day press upon thee
    With its crosses and its cares:
Then, though all the joys should leave thee
    To which human hearts will cling,
Thou shalt find a certain shelter
    Underneath Our Father's wing.

Printed by JOSIAH ALLEN, Birmingham.